TOEIC

練習測驗（13）

聽力錄音QR碼（1~100題）

LISTENING TEST

In the Listening test, you will be asked to demonstrate how well you understand spoken English. The entire Listening test will last approximately 45 minutes. There are four parts, and directions are given for each part. You must mark your answers on the separate answer sheet. Do not write your answers in your test book.

PART 1

Directions: For each question in this part, you will hear four statements about a picture in your test book. When you hear the statements, you must select the one statement that best describes what you see in the picture. Then find the number of the question on your answer sheet and mark your answer. The statements will not be printed in your test book and will be spoken only one time.

Statement (C), "They're sitting at a table," is the best description of the picture, so you should select answer (C) and mark it on your answer sheet.

1.

2.

GO ON TO THE NEXT PAGE.

3.

4.

5.

6.

GO ON TO THE NEXT PAGE.

PART 2

Directions: You will hear a question or statement and three responses spoken in English. They will not be printed in your test book and will be spoken only one time. Select the best response to the question or statement and mark the letter (A), (B), or (C) on your answer sheet.

7. Mark your answer on your answer sheet.

8. Mark your answer on your answer sheet.

9. Mark your answer on your answer sheet.

10. Mark your answer on your answer sheet.

11. Mark your answer on your answer sheet.

12. Mark your answer on your answer sheet.

13. Mark your answer on your answer sheet.

14. Mark your answer on your answer sheet.

15. Mark your answer on your answer sheet.

16. Mark your answer on your answer sheet.

17. Mark your answer on your answer sheet.

18. Mark your answer on your answer sheet.

19. Mark your answer on your answer sheet.

20. Mark your answer on your answer sheet.

21. Mark your answer on your answer sheet.

22. Mark your answer on your answer sheet.

23. Mark your answer on your answer sheet.

24. Mark your answer on your answer sheet.

25. Mark your answer on your answer sheet.

26. Mark your answer on your answer sheet.

27. Mark your answer on your answer sheet.

28. Mark your answer on your answer sheet.

29. Mark your answer on your answer sheet.

30. Mark your answer on your answer sheet.

31. Mark your answer on your answer sheet.

Directions: You will hear some conversations between two people. You will be asked to answer three questions about what the speakers say in each conversation. Select the best response to each question and mark the letter (A), (B), (C), or (D) on your answer sheet. The conversation will not be printed in your test book and will be spoken only one time.

32. Who most likely is Ms. Reagan?
(A) A travel agent.
(B) A bank clerk.
(C) A warehouse supervisor.
(D) A restaurant manager.

33. What is the man complaining about?
(A) An order has not arrived.
(B) A bill is not accurate.
(C) An item has been discontinued.
(D) A reservation was lost.

34. What does the manager say she will do?
(A) Delete an account.
(B) Speak to an employee.
(C) Refund a purchase.
(D) Confirm an address.

35. Who are the speakers?
(A) Teacher and student.
(B) Employee and customer.
(C) Doctor and patient.
(D) Friend and foe.

36. Where is this conversation most likely taking place?
(A) In an office.
(B) In a cafeteria.
(C) On a bus.
(D) At a business meeting.

37. What does the man ask for?
(A) An onion bagel.
(B) Extra sugar in the coffee.
(C) Extra cream cheese on the bagel.
(D) Hot coffee.

38. What is the man's problem?
(A) His schedule is too full.
(B) His computer isn't working.
(C) His confidence is shattered.
(D) His secretary is on vacation.

39. What will the man do tomorrow at three o'clock?
(A) Buy a new computer.
(B) Meet with a client.
(C) Leave for a business trip.
(D) Contact customer service.

40. What will Mary most likely do next?
(A) Find someone to fix Rex's computer.
(B) Cancel the meeting with Cooper.
(C) meet with Cooper and his associates.
(D) Fix Rex's computer herself.

41. What is the woman's problem?
(A) She lost her driver's license.
(B) She lost her wallet.
(C) She lost her cell phone.
(D) She lost her ATM card.

42. What does the man ask?
(A) Where it happened.
(B) How it happened.
(C) When it happened.
(D) Why it happened.

43. What will the speakers most likely do next?
(A) Make a phone call.
(B) Drive to the shopping mall.
(C) Walk to the bank.
(D) Try another ATM.

GO ON TO THE NEXT PAGE.

44. What are the speakers discussing?
    (A) Lunch.
    (B) The woman's boss.
    (C) Former clients.
    (D) A shortcut to the cafeteria.

45. What does the woman imply?
    (A) She's not hungry.
    (B) She's already had lunch.
    (C) She's unable to leave her desk.
    (D) She's happy with her job.

46. Where does the man work?
    (A) In sales.
    (B) In marketing.
    (C) In accounting.
    (D) In tech support.

47. What did Norman do?
    (A) He moved around on stage.
    (B) He grew up quickly.
    (C) He gave a performance.
    (D) He left too soon.

48. What does the woman ask?
    (A) Where did Norman learn his skill?
    (B) Where did Norman grow up?
    (C) When did Norman take lessons?
    (D) What was Norman's family like?

49. What is implied about Norman?
    (A) He's arrogant.
    (B) He's a musician.
    (C) He's from a foreign country.
    (D) He's ashamed of his skill.

50. In which department do the speakers work?
    (A) Accounting.
    (B) Public Relations.
    (C) Human Resources.
    (D) Marketing.

51. What does Caroline Wright ask for?
    (A) An instruction manual.
    (B) A password.
    (C) Some survey results.
    (D) A telephone number.

52. What does the man suggest that the women do?
    (A) Organize an event.
    (B) Drive to work together.
    (C) Share a workspace.
    (D) Submit a resume.

53. What are the speakers discussing?
    (A) Company gossip.
    (B) Study habits.
    (C) Political theory.
    (D) Vacation time.

54. What does the woman ask the man?
    (A) If he plans on leaving the company.
    (B) If he has spoken to Ben recently.
    (C) If he knows anything about a rumor.
    (D) If he wants to have lunch.

55. What does the man imply?
    (A) He has low status within the company.
    (B) He doesn't pay attention to gossip.
    (C) He has a close relationship with Ben.
    (D) He might be the source of the rumor.

56. Where is this conversation taking place?
    (A) At an auto repair shop.
    (B) At a discount grocery.
    (C) At a metal processing factory.
    (D) At a busy intersection.

57. What kind of problem does the woman have?
    (A) Auto-immune.
    (B) Auto-pilot.
    (C) Automotive.
    (D) Automatic.

58. What will the speakers most likely do next?
    (A) Sign a contract.
    (B) Inspect the woman's car.
    (C) Shake hands and call it a deal.
    (D) Watch a video about automobile maintenance.

59. Why is Bill Rubin being transferred to Oslo?
  - (A) To become director of European operations.
  - (B) To placate Chinese investors.
  - (C) To increase sales in London.
  - (D) To assist Brent Hines.

60. Where did Bill Rubin double revenues?
  - (A) Shanghai.
  - (B) London.
  - (C) Oslo.
  - (D) Paris.

61. What does the man imply?
  - (A) Norway is extremely cold in winter.
  - (B) Shanghai would have been a better fit.
  - (C) London won't miss him.
  - (D) Oslo is flooded.

---

62. Where are the speakers?
  - (A) In school.
  - (B) On a television set.
  - (C) In a hotel.
  - (D) On a journey.

63. What is the man's problem?
  - (A) His room is too cold.
  - (B) He would like to order room service.
  - (C) The television isn't working.
  - (D) The walls are too thin.

64. What does the woman say she will do?
  - (A) Replace the television in the man's room.
  - (B) Send someone to solve the man's problem.
  - (C) Reset the cable television system.
  - (D) Move the man to a different room.

---

65. What are the speakers talking about?
  - (A) A smart phone application.
  - (B) Computer tablets.
  - (C) Music players.
  - (D) Digital cameras.

66. What problem does the man mention?
  - (A) Customer testing has been delayed.
  - (B) Costs have been higher than estimated.
  - (C) There has been a shortage of parts.
  - (D) Some software is not working properly.

67. What does the man mean by //"Absolutely, Ms. Barrymore."//?
  - (A) He will provide a report.
  - (B) He will hire more programmers.
  - (C) He believes the problem has been resolved.
  - (D) He accepts responsibility for the mistake.

---

68. What does the man ask the woman?
  - (A) If she wants him to change the light in the hallway closet.
  - (B) If she reorganized the hallway closet.
  - (C) If she is planning on changing the light in the hallway closet.
  - (D) If she noticed the light is burned out in the hallway closet.

69. What does the woman say?
  - (A) That she didn't notice the light is out.
  - (B) That she was going to ask the man to change it.
  - (C) That she is going out to buy light bulbs.
  - (D) That she is concerned about saving energy.

70. What will the man most likely do next?
  - (A) Change the light bulb in the hallway closet.
  - (B) Go down to the hardware store.
  - (C) Ask the woman to change the light bulb in the hallway closet.
  - (D) Change all the light bulbs in the house.

GO ON TO THE NEXT PAGE.

Directions: You will hear some talks given by a single speaker. You will be asked to answer three questions about what the speaker says in each talk. Select the best response to each question and mark the letter (A), (B), (C), or (D) on your answer sheet. The talks will not be printed in your test book and will be spoken only one time.

71. What is true about Kurt Black?
    (A) He founded Center City.
    (B) His paintings are famous all over the world.
    (C) He comes from a family of artists.
    (D) His statue of William Center was self-financed.

72. What will Kurt Black talk about?
    (A) William Center.
    (B) The carving of the statue.
    (C) Portrait photography.
    (D) New York Institute of Art.

73. Who paid for the project?
    (A) William Center.
    (B) The Center City Cultural Foundation.
    (C) Kurt Black.
    (D) The New York Institute of Art.

74. What is the main purpose of this talk?
    (A) To inform.
    (B) To accuse.
    (C) To sell.
    (D) To oppose.

75. What does the speaker suggest?
    (A) Washing hands frequently.
    (B) Using cold water.
    (C) Using the dry cycle of the dishwasher.
    (D) Sterilizing all food used in the kitchen.

76. What is required for sanitizing?
    (A) Raw meat or fish.
    (B) 170°F.
    (C) Glassware.
    (D) Sponges.

77. Who is most likely the speaker?
    (A) A corporate manager.
    (B) A sales clerk.
    (C) A cashier.
    (D) A parking lot attendant.

78. What is the speaker talking about?
    (A) A shipping company.
    (B) A parking garage.
    (C) A marketing agency.
    (D) A retail store.

79. Which of the following is NOT an employee benefit?
    (A) Generous salaries.
    (B) Monthly bonuses.
    (C) A retirement plan.
    (D) Free parking.

80. Where was this report most likely being broadcast?
    (A) Radio.
    (B) Internet.
    (C) Television.
    (D) Public Address system.

81. What happened at Mount Holyoke?
    (A) A baseball game.
    (B) A forest fire.
    (C) A thunderstorm.
    (D) A traffic jam.

82. What will most likely happen tonight?
    (A) The Dodgers will go to Seattle.
    (B) The fire will be contained.
    (C) The skies will clear up.
    (D) The storm front will bring rain.

83. What is the main purpose of this announcement?
  (A) To promote a business.
  (B) To solicit charity donations.
  (C) To explain a policy.
  (D) To remind someone of an appointment.

84. When are the trucks scheduled to be deployed?
  (A) Monday through Friday.
  (B) Anytime before five p.m.
  (C) On Tuesday the 15th.
  (D) Throughout the month.

85. What is not accepted?
  (A) Household utensils.
  (B) Large appliances.
  (C) Used clothing.
  (D) Cookware.

---

86. Who is the speaker most likely to be?
  (A) A successful investment broker.
  (B) A sleep therapist.
  (C) An author of folk tales.
  (D) A serial killer.

87. What does the speaker say about the stock market?
  (A) It is lethal.
  (B) It is risky.
  (C) It is sleepy.
  (D) It is folksy.

88. How does the speaker measure the risk of his investments?
  (A) By hand.
  (B) By how much money he makes or loses.
  (C) By keeping track of his fortunes.
  (D) By how much sleep he loses worrying about them.

---

89. Who is being introduced?
  (A) An elderly beer maker.
  (B) A famous politician.
  (C) A corporate executive.
  (D) A young entrepreneur.

90. What will the speaker talk about?
  (A) His education.
  (B) His business.
  (C) His religion.
  (D) His family.

91. When can the audience ask questions?
  (A) At the end of the speech.
  (B) Before the speech begins.
  (C) 30 minutes later.
  (D) There will be no questions allowed.

---

92. Where does this announcement take place?
  (A) On the radio.
  (B) At a business meeting.
  (C) On television.
  (D) In a bus station.

93. What caused the 7-1-8 bus to be late?
  (A) A snow storm in Denver.
  (B) Heavy traffic in Los Angeles.
  (C) Mechanical trouble on the outskirts of the city.
  (D) Parades in Las Vegas.

94. What should listeners do if they want a refund?
  (A) Take the 7-1-8 bus to Las Vegas.
  (B) Bring their boarding passes to customer service.
  (C) Have lunch in the lounge.
  (D) Complain to the manager.

GO ON TO THE NEXT PAGE.

Item	Original Price	Sale Price
Dining room table	$100.00	$25.00
Coffee table	$54.00	$18.00
Patio table	$90.00	$30.00
Kitchen table	$110.00	$27.50

95. Look at the graphic. What is the sale price of the table being described?
(A) $18.00.
(B) $25.00.
(C) $27.50.
(D) $30.00.

96. According to the speaker, why do customers like the table?
(A) It is hand-made.
(B) It is available in many colors.
(C) It is easy to assemble.
(D) It is inexpensive.

97. What does the speaker say can be found on a website?
(A) Some instructions.
(B) Some recipes.
(C) A warranty.
(D) A coupon.

CHARLOTTESVILLE WEEKEND WEATHER FORECAST			
Thursday	Friday	Saturday	Sunday
Cloudy and humid	Partly cloudy with scattered thunderstorms	Extreme heat advisory	Sunny with onshore winds
Hi: 95 / Lo: 78	Hi: 97 / Lo: 83	Hi: 103 / Lo: 88	Hi: 96 / Lo: 80

98. What event is being discussed?
(A) A grand opening.
(B) A charity walk.
(C) A trip to the zoo.
(D) A music festival.

99. Look at the graphic. Which day was the event originally scheduled for?
(A) Thursday.
(B) Friday.
(C) Saturday.
(D) Sunday.

100. What does the speaker ask the listener to do?
(A) Arrange a meeting.
(B) Contact scheduled performers.
(C) Rent industrial fans.
(D) Print new tickets.

This is the end of the Listening test. Turn to Part 5 in your test book.

READING TEST

In the Reading test, you will read a variety of texts and answer several different types of reading comprehension questions. The entire Reading test will last 75 minutes. There are three parts, and directions are given for each part. You are encouraged to answer as many questions as possible within the time allowed.

You must mark your answers on the separate answer sheet. Do not write your answers in your test book.

PART 5

Directions: A word or phrase is missing in each of the sentences below. Four answer choices are given below each sentence. Select the best answer to complete the sentence. Then mark the letter (A), (B), (C), or (D) on your answer sheet.

101. Do you know when the boss is ------- New York?
- (A) going at
- (B) come to
- (C) leaving for
- (D) arrived in

102. The winning lottery numbers will be announced at -------.
- (A) seven o'clock
- (B) seventeen
- (C) the seventh
- (D) the seven

103. Researchers have ------- determined whether playing video games changes the brain's chemistry.
- (A) yet
- (B) not yet
- (C) while
- (D) not while

104. The clerk's job is to handle cash -------.
- (A) transformations
- (B) transportations
- (C) transactions
- (D) transplantations

105. I'm sorry, sir, but I can't give you a refund without a -------.
- (A) statement
- (B) reference
- (C) bill
- (D) receipt

106. The news of Ronald's recovery brought a smile ------- my face.
- (A) in
- (B) on
- (C) by
- (D) to

107. No one knows how long it will take to ------- the wildfires in Arizona.
- (A) malnourish
- (B) distinguish
- (C) extinguish
- (D) establish

108. The bus will ------- in front of the library entrance.
- (A) throw us up
- (B) stick us around
- (C) drop us off
- (D) pick us apart

GO ON TO THE NEXT PAGE.

109. Don't take what Jim says at -------. He's been known to stretch the truth.
   (A) face value
   (B) a discount
   (C) shelf life
   (D) great risk

110. We need to contact our supplier. ------- the call when you have a minute.
   (A) Take
   (B) Make
   (C) Give
   (D) Place

111. Let's try that hotel down the street. This one is fully -------.
   (A) set
   (B) acquired
   (C) booked
   (D) close

112. James is far ------- home and feeling lonely.
   (A) at
   (B) of
   (C) with
   (D) from

113. It's your first time. There's nothing shameful about ------- nervous.
   (A) to be
   (B) has been
   (C) being
   (D) you're

114. He was determined to let nothing ------- of his success.
   (A) go by the book
   (B) fall by the wayside
   (C) get in the way
   (D) look for an outlet

115. ------- both sides agree to settle the dispute, there's no guarantee the truce will last.
   (A) Only if
   (B) Provided that
   (C) Even
   (D) Even if

116. Excuse me, miss. There ------- be a fly in my soup.
   (A) seemed
   (B) seemingly
   (C) apparently
   (D) appears to

117. You need to register in order to open an e-mail -------.
   (A) setting
   (B) file
   (C) account
   (D) direction

118. The man ------- spilled his coffee.
   (A) by accident
   (B) accidentally
   (C) designed to
   (D) with intention

119. Tim's illness seems to have -------. He's feeling much better now.
   (A) borne in mind
   (B) run its course
   (C) revolved around
   (D) lightened his load

120. The maestro's performance received mixed -------.
   (A) tests
   (B) studies
   (C) essays
   (D) reviews

121. Many supermarkets are now providing customers with ------- checkout lanes, eliminating the need for cashiers.
(A) self-esteem
(B) self-styled
(C) self-taught
(D) self-service

122. Would you mind ------- late tonight?
(A) stayed
(B) stay
(C) staying
(D) stays

123. In order to play any game, first you must understand the -------.
(A) runes
(B) rulers
(C) rules
(D) rumors

124. I'm really excited about our ski trip this weekend. I can't wait to ------- the slopes!
(A) hug
(B) hold
(C) house
(D) hit

125. The saying goes that you can't make a(n) ------- without breaking eggs.
(A) baby
(B) record
(C) omelet
(D) deal

126. Skeptics say computer models used to predict global warming are ------- to error.
(A) pound
(B) pressed
(C) prone
(D) pure

127. The workers threatened to go on ------- if their demands were not met.
(A) trial
(B) maternity
(C) strike
(D) duty

128. After a thorough inspection, I found several potential safety hazards in my work area, which I reported to my -------.
(A) therapist
(B) supervisor
(C) dietitian
(D) auditor

129. Your exercise program may seem difficult now, but ------- and I promise you'll see positive results.
(A) stick with it
(B) drop it on
(C) seal it with
(D) it means it

130. I haven't spoken to my sister ------- September.
(A) from
(B) until
(C) by
(D) since

GO ON TO THE NEXT PAGE.

PART 6

Directions: Read the texts that follow. A word, phrase, or sentence is missing in parts of each text. Four answer choices are given below each of the texts. Select the best answer to complete the text. Then mark the letter (A), (B), (C), or (D) on your answer sheet.

Questions 131-134 refer to the news article.

Computer Funds Approved by Board of Supervisors

THOUSAND OAKS (May 23) — New technology is coming -------
131.
the students of Thousand Oaks Unified School District. On Friday, Mayor Cheyenne Loomis announced that her "Future Now" proposal has been approved by the Board of Supervisors.

-------. The program allots $200,000 to each school in the city for the
132.
purchase of computers. Students will be allowed to take home laptops and tablets ------- for special assignments and class projects,
133.
but they will normally ------- to the students only during school hours.
134.

131. (A) to
(B) at
(C) from
(D) on

132. (A) The desks will be purchased at a discount rate
(B) The final decision is expected next month
(C) Nevertheless, the mayor remains content with the decision
(D) The vote took place on Wednesday, May 21

133. (A) occasionally
(B) exceptionally
(C) finally
(D) supposedly

134. (A) are available
(B) not available
(C) be available
(D) were availed

Questions 135-138 refer to the following advertisement.

THE AD AGENCY

Let's face it: Promoting your business can be frustrating. Trade shows and industry forums are ------- useful venues for meeting potential clients.
135.

-------, the Internet has become the most critical advertising and
136.
marketing outlet.

The Ad Agency utilizes both traditional commercial outlets and the Internet to promote clients' offerings. -------. In addition to exceptional
137.
traditional advertising, The Ad Agency has the expertise to help you to ------- your online presence. Why wait? Choose our award-winning firm
138.
to strengthen your company's image today!

---

135. (A) evenly
  (B) still
  (C) soon
  (D) nowhere

136. (A) However
  (B) To demonstrate
  (C) Otherwise
  (D) As a result

137. (A) Marketing professionals give conflicting advice
  (B) Traditional methods have the best impact
  (C) We can develop a diverse plan for your business
  (D) We have recently changed our terms of service

138. (A) optimal
  (B) optimum
  (C) optimization
  (D) optimize

GO ON TO THE NEXT PAGE.

IMPORTANT NEWS

FOR TOXXICO MANUFACTURING STAFF

We are pleased to announce that the installation of new sorting and packing equipment in our Sarasota Springs plant is now complete.

The new machines ------- work flow by allowing for complete
139.
flexibility in production without having to stop and retool.

With five sorting and three packing machines of ------- sizes, we
140.
expect to be able to fill a wider range of orders, from small to very large on short notice. This ------- is an important way to ensure that
141.
Toxxico Manufacturing continues to be a leader in the plastic fabrication industry.

-------. Geoff Monteith, who is managing this effort, will contact each
142.
of you soon with details.

---

139. (A) have been improved
(B) were improving
(C) will improve
(D) improvement

140. (A) vary
(B) varies
(C) varying
(D) variation

141. (A) contract
(B) upgrade
(C) proposal
(D) impression

142. (A) All personnel will be trained on the new equipment by the end of the month
(B) Supervisors completed a tour of the facilities yesterday
(C) Unfortunately, the installation fee cost more than we had anticipated
(D) As you are aware, our industry is increasingly competitive

OFFICE ORACLE SUPPLY CO.
established 1982

3589 W. Des Moines Avenue
Des Moines, IA 60034
(404) 243-0924

October 22
Ms. Clara Helms
World 2 Go Travel
901 W. Harper Street
Cedar Rapids, IA 60034

Dear Ms. Helms,

Thank you for your purchase of 10 Magenta ABS Plastic Cartridges for CubePro 3D Printers from Office Oracle Supply Co. Your online order was received on November 1 and is ready for shipping. -------.
143.

We appreciate that you have chosen Office Oracle for your company's clerical and office needs. As a show of thanks, we are applying a 10 percent discount to this ------- order. -------, we are including a reimbursement of shipping charges.
144.   **145.**

Enclosed you will find the adjusted invoice and a check for $124.00.

Office Oracle is pleased to welcome you to the family and ------- to providing you
146.

with quality products and service in the future.

Sincerely,
John Stevenson
Customer Service Representative

---

143. (A) Your interest in employment opportunities with us is appreciated
(B) Unfortunately, we are writing to inform you of a delay in delivery
(C) However, it seems that you have failed to reply
(D) You may expect to receive your order in 5-7 days

144. (A) ongoing
(B) complimentary
(C) particular
(D) sequential

145. (A) For example
(B) Still
(C) However
(D) Additionally

146. (A) leaves room
(B) looks forward
(C) goes back
(D) pushes harder

GO ON TO THE NEXT PAGE.

PART 7

Directions: In this part you will read a selection of texts, such as magazine and newspaper articles, e-mails, and instant messages. Each text or set of texts is followed by several questions. Select the best answer for each question and mark the letter (A), (B), (C), or (D) on your answer sheet.

Questions 147-148 refer to the following article.

In an effort to curb residents' unhealthy eating habits, Denmark has introduced a new tax on foods that contain more than 2.3 percent saturated fat. The "fat tax," generally regarded to be the first of its kind in the world, will raise the prices of foods like butter, milk, cheese, pizza, meat, and oil. Still, some question whether the tax will actually deter people from buying the products, and others question whether saturated fat was the wisest food component to target, given that salt, sugar, and refined carbohydrates can also be detrimental to people's health. Danish officials say they hope the new tax will help limit the population's intake of fatty foods. However, some consumers have begun hoarding to beat the price rise, and some producers have called the tax an outrage. Others say that they, like many other Danes, have already started shopping abroad to avoid the tax.

147. What is true about the "fat tax"?
(A) It applies to all Danish food products.
(B) It will cause more people to get fat.
(C) It is probably the first of its kind in the world.
(D) It targets the most unhealthy food choices.

148. Which of the following has not been a result of the "fat tax"?
(A) Danish citizens have lost more weight.
(B) Producers have complained.
(C) Consumers have begun hoarding supplies.
(D) Some consumers are altering their shopping habits to avoid the tax.

City of Darien SEA DEVILS Swim School

20% OFF all Spring Session NEW Client Swim School Enrollments

Must present voucher to redeem offer.
Offer valid until July 1

Not vaild with any other offer. Subject to terms and availability.

149. What is being advertised?
(A) A charity drive for children.
(B) A group discount on soda.
(C) A promotion for pizza.
(D) A swim school.

150. Who is eligible to use the coupon?
(A) Anyone after July 1.
(B) New clients.
(C) Poor swimmers.
(D) Existing clients.

GO ON TO THE NEXT PAGE.

Memorandum

TO: GTS Sales staff

FROM: Karen Moore

DATE: April 18

SUBJECT: Customer Presentation

The JSKL Marketing presentation you prepared last week to showcase our new product line was exceptional!

Your enthusiasm, sales strategy, and product knowledge were impressive and certainly sealed the deal with Mr. Lockhart!

Thank you for your outstanding work and dedication. Bonus checks will be distributed next week.

My sincere congratulations to all of you!

151. Who gave the sales presentation?
(A) Karen Moore.
(B) Mr. Lockhart.
(C) The GTS sales staff.
(D) The JSKL marketing team.

152. What will happen next week?
(A) Mr. Lockhart will visit the office.
(B) Karen Moore will resign.
(C) JSKL will sign a contract.
(D) The GTS sales staff will receive bonus checks.

WILD WILLIE'S USED CARS

SPRING BONANZA LIQUIDATION SALE

NO DEPOSIT! NO PAYMENT UNTIL 2019!

THIS IS WILD WILLIE'S CRAZIEST DEAL EVER

- 48 month financing at low rates
- FREE comprehensive mechanical warranty
- FREE Roadside Assistance program

CHECK OUT OUR LATEST ARRIVALS

2013	Mercedes-Benz E650 10K miles, one owner, spotless	15,550
2013	BMW M4 15K miles, convertible, metallic gray	13,330
2014	Lexus L300 7K miles, ABS, GPS, loaded	12,000
2015	Tesla Roadster 10K miles, electric, gas miser	22,000
2015	Mercedes-Benz E180 4.5K miles, factory trade-in	24,440
2016	Porsche 911 Turbo, 2K miles, showroom model, nice!	33,330

153. What is this advertisement for?
(A) Roadside Assistance.
(B) A sale on used cars.
(C) New Cars.
(D) An automotive warranty.

154. Which of the following is NOT offered by the ad?
(A) 48 month financing.
(B) No deposit.
(C) Free warranty.
(D) No payment.

GO ON TO THE NEXT PAGE.

Questions 155-157 refer to the following advertisement.

Date posted: June 6   Views: 249   Replies: 198

❂ $3100/2BR DOWNTOWN OAKLAND APARTMENT FOR RENT — (Lake Merritt BART)

A spacious two-bedroom apartment in the Essex on Lake Merritt will be ready for a new tenant on July 1. It is conveniently located across from the Lake Merritt BART station, giving residents quick access to the San Francisco business district and many other destinations in the Bay Area. It is a leisurely walk to popular nightlife options and dining establishments in the Uptown area. Vacancies in this highly desirable residence are rare. The unit is located on the 18th floor and has a large terrace. Located on a relatively quiet and peaceful street, the Essex soars above the other buildings in the neighborhood, so it is full of natural light as well. The unit has beautiful hardwood flooring and a contemporary kitchen with energy-efficient appliances. One designated parking space in the underground garage is included. The Essex on Lake Merritt residents receive a substantial discount at the Kinetic Fitness Center located in the shopping center adjacent to the building. The apartment will be open for tours this weekend, June 8-10. Rent is $3,100 per month. A one-time deposit of $9,300 is also required. This deposit and the first month's rent are due upon signing of the rental agreement.

To apply, please e-mail vacancy@essexproperties.com

155. What is suggested about the apartment?
(A) It was recently remodeled.
(B) It is close to restaurants.
(C) It is on the top floor of the building.
(D) It is fully furnished.

156. What is included with the apartment?
(A) A transit pass.
(B) A cleaning service.
(C) A fitness club membership.
(D) A parking space.

157. What is indicated about the Essex on Lake Merritt?
(A) It is in the center of the business district.
(B) It has several shops in the lobby.
(C) It is taller than the other buildings in the area.
(D) It currently has many unoccupied apartments.

INTERNSHIP (PAID)
Recruitment, HR, and Training Support

With 60 restaurants and food service operations on both the East and West Coasts, PRG offers world-class dining experiences. The East Coast corporate office is looking for a bright, energetic individual to support the East Coast HR department.

Responsibilities:
• Supporting the recruitment manager and the recruiting process.
• Working with the Training Manager.
• Managing recruitment, orientation and training materials.
• Drafting, revising and posting job ads on a weekly basis.
• Running errands for the reception desk if needed.

Requirements:
• Currently enrolled or graduated from a hospitality or business school and interested in HR.
• Meticulous attention to detail.
• Solid writing skills and ability to communicate effectively with all levels of management.
• Interest in food a plus.
• Strong knowledge of MS Word preferred but not required.

Interested candidates may apply online at: www.PatinaGroup.com

158. Who might be interested in this position?
(A) Recent college graduates.
(B) High school students.
(C) Someone who hates writing.
(D) Spanish teachers.

159. What is preferred but not required?
(A) A strong background in the Arts.
(B) An interest in cooking.
(C) A strong knowledge of MS Word.
(D) Experience working with the disabled.

160. Where is this job opening located?
(A) The West Coast corporate office.
(B) The East Coast HR department.
(C) A restaurant on the West Coast.
(D) A reception desk on the East Coast.

GO ON TO THE NEXT PAGE.

Beneath the world's oceans lie rugged mountains, active volcanoes, vast plateaus and almost bottomless trenches. The deepest ocean trenches could easily swallow up the tallest mountains on land.

Around most continents are shallow seas that cover gently sloping areas called continental shelves. These reach depths of about 650 feet (200 m). The continental shelves end at the steeper continental slopes, which lead down to the deepest parts of the ocean.

Beyond the continental slope is the abyss. The abyss contains plains, long mountain ranges called ocean ridges, isolated mountains called seamounts, and ocean trenches, which are the deepest parts of the oceans. In the centers of some ocean ridges are long rift valleys, where earthquakes and volcanic eruptions are common. Some volcanoes that rise from the ridges appear above the surface as islands.

Other mountain ranges are made up of extinct volcanoes. Some seamounts, called guyots, are extinct volcanoes with flat tops. Scientists think that these underwater mountains were once islands but their tops were worn away by waves.

161. What is this article mainly about?
(A) Mountain ranges.
(B) Earthquakes.
(C) The oceans.
(D) Volcanoes.

162. What are guyots?
(A) Extinct underwater volcanoes.
(B) Long rift valleys.
(C) Active earthquakes.
(D) Continental slopes.

163. What is true about the abyss?
(A) It is located on top of the continental slope.
(B) It contains the deepest parts of the ocean.
(C) It swallows other mountain ranges.
(D) It produces the shallow seas.

Baltimore, Maryland, has a very long and rich history. It is perhaps best known for being the site of the historic Battle of Baltimore during the War of 1812. Over the course of the battle, British invaders bombed Fort McHenry with rockets as Francis Scott Key wrote, "The Star-Spangled Banner," which would become the American national anthem. Baltimore was also the site of the first casualty of the American Civil War.

Baltimore also has a large African-American population that has played an important role in its history. African-Americans have had a major presence in Baltimore since the Revolutionary War. During that time they were brought to Baltimore as slaves from Africa. Baltimore was also one of the hotbeds during the American Civil Rights movement and famous African-Americans such as Thurgood Marshall and Kweisi Mfume have made Baltimore their hometown. R&B artists such as Tupac Shakur, Dru Hill and Mario have also emerged from Baltimore. Currently, African-Americans form a majority (within the city limits) at 64%.

164. According to the report, what is Baltimore best known for?
(A) Barbeque ribs.
(B) R&B music.
(C) Being the site of a historic battle in the War of 1812.
(D) As the hometown of Thurgood Marshall.

165. What famous song was written in Baltimore?
(A) "Ridin' Dirty," by Tupac.
(B) "The Star-Spangled Banner" by Francis Scott Key.
(C) "America, the Beautiful" by Dru Hill.
(D) "Blowin' in the Wind," by Bob Dylan.

166. What is true about African-Americans in Baltimore?
(A) They bombed Fort McHenry.
(B) They started the Civil Rights Movement.
(C) They prefer R&B to all other kinds of music.
(D) They form a majority within the city limits.

167. How long have African-Americans had a major presence in Baltimore?
(A) Since slavery ended in the United States.
(B) Since the War of 1812.
(C) Since the American Revolutionary War.
(D) Since the Civil Rights Movement.

GO ON TO THE NEXT PAGE.

Economic theory suggests that individuals place some value on their time. When it comes to walking, time to destination can be minimized by walking more quickly. Unlike other possible determinants of preferred walking speed, which become less favorable at higher speeds, time to destination becomes more favorable (less time spent walking) with increasing speed. Value of time therefore likely represents a key factor influencing preferred walking speed.

Scientists from Sweden measured preferred walking speeds of urban pedestrians in 31 countries and found that walking speed is positively correlated with the country's per capita GDP and purchasing power parity, as well as with a measure of individualism in the country's society. People living in more affluent places and therefore with higher economic values to their time generally walk more quickly.

This idea is broadly consistent with common intuition. Everyday situations often change the value of time. For example, when walking to catch a bus, arriving marginally after the bus has left may result in a relatively long wait. Here, the value of the one minute immediately before the bus has departed may be worth 30 minutes of time (the time saved not waiting for the next bus). The idea of hurrying to catch a bus has become almost a cliché. Supporting this idea, individuals who are "hurried" under experimental conditions are less likely to stop in response to a distraction and arrive at their destination sooner.

168. What does the article suggest?
(A) People living in more affluent places generally walk more quickly.
(B) Modern walking speed is based on personal preference.
(C) Personal income has no influence on walking speed.
(D) Individualism is the sole determinant for preferred walking speed.

169. What is the article based on?
(A) Urban legend.
(B) Popular opinion.
(C) Common intuition.
(D) Scientific research.

170. What is this article mainly about?
(A) The relationship between walking speed and value of time.
(B) The preferred walking speed of individuals.
(C) The concept of common intuition.
(D) The key factors which determine GDP.

171. Which of the following is NOT a key factor influencing preferred walking speed?
(A) Value of time.
(B) Purchasing power parity.
(C) Individual freedom.
(D) Experimental conditions.

Nearly half of China's wealthiest citizens are considering emigrating, with the United States and Canada the most popular destinations, according to a new report from the authors of China's rich list. The survey by the Bank of China and the Hurun Report, which publishes luxury magazines and runs a research institute, found that 46 percent of Chinese with assets worth more than 10 million yuan ($1.6 million) were considering moving abroad. Another 14 percent had already begun the process, it said. Many said they were seeking a better education for their children and cited concerns about the security of their assets in China. Nearly a third of the respondents said they already had investments overseas, in many cases to enable them to emigrate. Some countries offer residency to foreign citizens who are prepared to invest large sums.

High inflation and the difficulty of investing overseas were also cited in the survey, which took in 980 people in 18 Chinese cities. More than 30 years of booming economic growth have allowed some Chinese to build up vast fortunes once unthinkable in the nominally communist nation. China now has 271 dollar billionaires, according to Hurun's 2017 rich list, up from 189 last year, despite the global economic crisis. The latest report said that 960,000 people in China are now worth more than 10 million yuan, up by 9.7 percent from 2016. Many of the country's wealthiest citizens have made their money in China's construction and property sectors, as well as a growing domestic retail market. But the rigid education system, rising living costs and widespread corruption have led many to look for homes abroad.

GO ON TO THE NEXT PAGE.

172. What is this report based on?

   (A) Results of a laboratory experiment.

   (B) The author's personal opinion.

   (C) Classified government documents.

   (D) A survey of 980 rich people in China.

173. What does the report say?

   (A) Corruption in China has led to a widening gap between the rich and poor.

   (B) The Chinese education system is slowly catching up to Western counterparts.

   (C) Nearly half of China's wealthiest citizens want to live somewhere else.

   (D) China has more billionaires per capita than any other country in the world.

174. What does the report suggest?

   (A) Individual wealth is a relatively new phenomenon in China.

   (B) Nobody is safe from the Chinese government.

   (C) Life in the United States is infinitely better than anywhere else in the world.

   (D) China's real estate bubble will eventually burst.

175. What does the survey say?

   (A) Over half of respondents cited education as a reason for wanting to leave.

   (B) Nearly a third of respondents say they already have investments overseas.

   (C) The majority of Chinese billionaires made their fortunes the old fashioned way.

   (D) Approximately a million people are now considered dollar millionaires in China.

JACKSON LIGHTING SUPPLY
1234 First Avenue
Scranton, Pennsylvania
Phone (234)555-5555
On the web: http://www.jax.supply.com

Dear Valued Customer,

Due to the rise in raw material costs led by fuel and other commodities and various other operating expenses, we must unfortunately raise the cost of our products to you.

While we have made every effort to avoid raising our prices, we are no longer able to absorb all increases and as such will be applying a price increase of 10% for our products. Please be aware that changes in our business model and on-going investments in equipment and technology have enabled us to provide products and terms that support market requirements and keep increases to a minimum.

This increase will allow us to continue to provide you the complete range of quality products and services you've come to depend on from Jackson Lighting Supply.

Please review our new price list, which takes effect with orders placed on or after November 1. Also note that any existing orders will be honored at your current prices.

We want to thank you for your valued business and continued support during these difficult times. We really appreciate your understanding regarding the necessity for this price increase.

If you have any queries regarding this change then please don't hesitate to contact me.

Sincerely,
Don Jackson

GO ON TO THE NEXT PAGE.

NEW PRICE LIST AS OF NOVEMBER 1

Item/Description	Previous Price	New Price
Altman 6" Scoop	12.50	13.75
Altman 6" Fresnel	13.00	14.30
Altman Par 64	9.00	9.90
Altman Par 40 Strip	8.00	8.80
MBT Par 36	3.00	3.30
MBT Par 36 Color Wheel	7.00	7.70
MBT Source	11.50	12.65
MBT Iris	11.50	12.65
ETC 10 Degree	10.00	11.00
ETC 16 Degree	12.00	13.20
ETC Ellipsoidal	22.00	24.20
Philips Par 4/8/16	4.00	4.40
Philips Par 32	6.00	6.60
Philips 6" Scoop	11.75	12.92
Philips 6" Fresnel	12.25	13.47
Philips R40 Ellipsoidal	20.00	22.00

176. What is the main purpose of the letter?
- (A) To place an order.
- (B) To request an action.
- (C) To explain a price increase.
- (D) To demand a refund.

177. What does the author ask the recipient to do?
- (A) Reorder their supplies.
- (B) Change their business model.
- (C) Deliver and install a product.
- (D) Contact the author if they have any questions.

178. What will happen to existing orders placed before November 1?
- (A) The orders will be cancelled.
- (B) The orders will be honored at existing prices.
- (C) The orders will be filled by a different company.
- (D) The orders will be processed at the new prices.

179. What does Jackson Lighting Supply most likely sell?
- (A) Cameras.
- (B) Hand tools.
- (C) Light bulbs.
- (D) Party Supplies.

180. James placed an order for 10 Altman Par 40 Strips on October 29. How much did Jackson Lighting Supply charge him?
- (A) $30.00.
- (B) $33.00.
- (C) $80.00.
- (D) $88.00.

GO ON TO THE NEXT PAGE.

Article 1

Signs that the Earth is warming have been recorded all over the globe. The easiest way to see increasing temperatures is through the thermometer records kept over the past century and a half. Around the world, the Earth's average temperature has risen more than 1 degree Fahrenheit (0.8 degrees Celsius) over the last century, and about twice that in parts of the Arctic.

Although we can't look at thermometers going back thousands of years, we do have some records that help us figure out what temperatures and concentrations were like in the distant past. For example, trees store information about the climate in the place where they live. Each year, trees grow thicker and form new rings. In warmer and wetter years, the rings are thicker. Old trees and wood can tell us about conditions hundreds or even several thousands of years ago.

Computer models help scientists to understand the Earth's climate, or long-term weather patterns. Models also allow scientists to make predictions about the future climate. Basically, models simulate how the atmosphere and oceans absorb energy from the sun and transport it around the globe. Factors that affect the amount of the sun's energy reaching Earth's surface are what drive the climate in these models, as in real life. These include things like greenhouse gases, particles in the atmosphere (such as from volcanoes), and changes in energy coming from the sun itself. And what these computer models are showing is that the Earth is steadily getting warmer.

Article 2

Many claim that global warming is obvious and that all arguments against it fail. The problem is that often what is "obvious" isn't always true. Concern over global warming is overblown and misdirected. Climate science is often reported as if computer models are facts. A computer model can not discriminate theories into true and false because it is not measuring reality. Such models may give one an idea where to experiment, but to claim they "prove" anything is pure fiction and should lead one to discount the source. At best you can use a computer model to disprove a theory.

All predictions of global warming are based on computer models, not historical data. Furthermore, satellite readings of the troposphere (the area where scientists say global warming will immediately appear) show no warming in the 23 years since these readings began. These readings are accurate to within 0.01 degrees Celsius and are consistent with data from weather balloons. Only land-based temperature stations show a warming trend, and these stations do not cover the entire planet, do not account for heat generated by nearby urban development, and are subject to human error.

The public needs to recognize that just because something is modeled on a computer, it does not necessarily represent reality, and the result of bad public policy can be expensive.

GO ON TO THE NEXT PAGE.

181. In what way do the two articles differ?

(A) Opinion.

(B) Length.

(C) Vocabulary.

(D) Subject matter.

182. In what way are the articles similar?

(A) They agree on the subject.

(B) They discuss the same subject.

(C) They blame the same person.

(D) Neither is based on fact.

183. According to the first article, what is true about the Earth?

(A) It is slowly getting colder.

(B) It is steadily getting warmer.

(C) It is obviously getting wetter.

(D) It is probably getting drier.

184. According to the second article, what are all predictions of global warming based on?

(A) Historical data.

(B) Tree rings.

(C) Computer models.

(D) Weather balloons.

185. What does the author of the second article imply?

(A) The general public is misinformed about global warming.

(B) Global warming can't be found in tree rings.

(C) Greenhouse gases have not contributed to global warming.

(D) Global warming might be real but no one can prove it.

MILTON BRADLEY THEATRE SET TO REOPEN

SPRINGFIELD, MA (April 8)—After many decades of groundbreaking performances and captivated audiences, the Milton Bradley Theatre was in great need of refurbishing.

Designed by Werner Rovitz in a post-modern style, the building was visually stunning when the theatre first opened, but it had begun to show its age. Although the theatre had retained its beauty over time, it was in need of some care to ensure that this beauty would endure into the future.

After an extensive renovation, the theatre has reopened. The grand chandelier and impressive murals in the lobby have been thoroughly cleaned, the seat cushions have been replaced and are now covered in a burgundy fabric, and the concession stands in the main lobby and on the balcony floor have been enlarged and remodeled. In addition, a new parking garage, the final part of the renovation project, is expected to be completed in September.

The reopening coincides with the 30th anniversary of the theatre's resident company, the Milton Bradley Players, whose next play is the world premiere of *The Last Centurion* by renowned playwright Benjamin Glass. The show will be directed by the theatre's own artistic director, Ocasio Del Potre.

by J. David Cromm

GO ON TO THE NEXT PAGE.

A FRIENDLY REMINDER FOR THEATRE PATRONS

Please turn off all electronic devices before the performance begins.

You are cordially invited to join us for an informal question-and-answer session with the director and cast immediately following the show. In honor of our 30th anniversary, we are offering audience members a chance to win a complimentary pass for two for next year's entire season!

This opportunity is available during all performances of *The Last Centurion* (April 18-May 15). Simply complete the form on page 27 of this program, tear it off, and place it in the box in the lobby during intermission or at the end of the show. A winner will be selected at random on May 15 and contacted by e-mail.

From:	Kristen Lawler <kLawler@funtech.com>
To:	Don Weinstein <dweinstein@mbtheater.com>
Re:	Congratulations! You're the Winner!
Date:	May 18

Dear Mr. Weinstein,

Thank you! It's such a wonderful feeling to have won a free season pass for two for the next season. For your information, I have attended dozens of shows at the Milton Bradley Theatre that I have enjoyed very much. I was particularly impressed by cast of *The Last Centurion*, and the Q&A session was exceptionally informative. Needless to say, I am looking forward to using my season pass. Thank you so much!

Sincerely,
Kristen Lawler

186. What is a purpose of the article?
  (A) To announce the reopening of a theater.
  (B) To review a theater company's recent performances.
  (C) To report changes to a theater's upcoming season.
  (D) To invite the public to a theater's anniversary party.

187. According to the article, what is scheduled to be ready in September?
  (A) A parking lot.
  (B) An adaptation of a play.
  (C) An expanded snack bar.
  (D) An education center.

188. According to the theater program insert, how can people enter the contest?
  (A) By e-mail.
  (B) By mailing a submission to the theater.
  (C) By depositing a form in the lobby.
  (D) By visiting the theater's website.

189. Who will address audience questions after the performance?
  (A) J. David Cromm.
  (B) Werner Rovitz.
  (C) Benjamin Glass.
  (D) Ocasio Del Potre.

190. What is suggested about Ms. Lawler?
  (A) She met Mr. Weinstein at an event in April.
  (B) She attended a performance of *The Last Centurion*.
  (C) She has ordered a ticket subscription for the next season.
  (D) She organized the question-and-answer session.

GO ON TO THE NEXT PAGE.

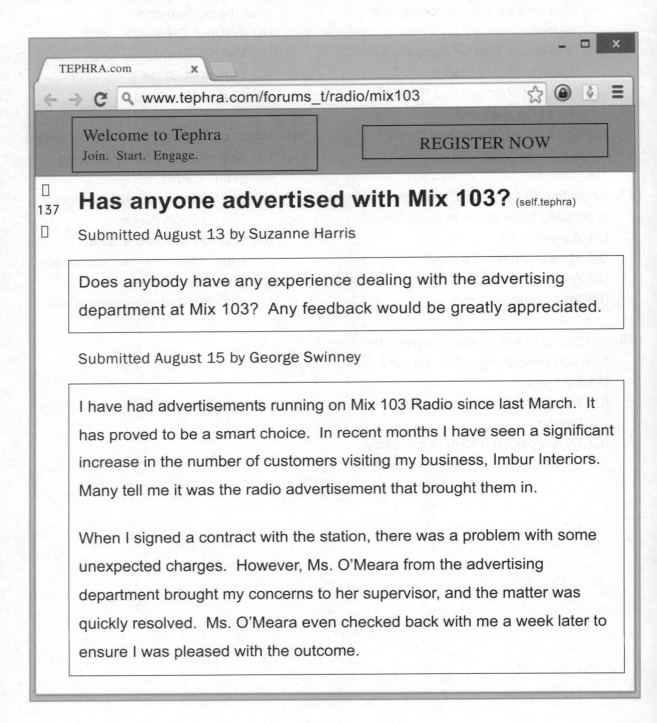

TEPHRA.com ×

www.tephra.com/forums_t/radio/mix103

Welcome to Tephra
Join. Start. Engage.

REGISTER NOW

137

Has anyone advertised with Mix 103? (self.tephra)

Submitted August 13 by Suzanne Harris

Does anybody have any experience dealing with the advertising department at Mix 103? Any feedback would be greatly appreciated.

Submitted August 15 by George Swinney

I have had advertisements running on Mix 103 Radio since last March. It has proved to be a smart choice. In recent months I have seen a significant increase in the number of customers visiting my business, Imbur Interiors. Many tell me it was the radio advertisement that brought them in.

When I signed a contract with the station, there was a problem with some unexpected charges. However, Ms. O'Meara from the advertising department brought my concerns to her supervisor, and the matter was quickly resolved. Ms. O'Meara even checked back with me a week later to ensure I was pleased with the outcome.

From:	Casey O'Meara
To:	All Staff
Re:	Final Broadcast
Date:	September 29

Dear All,

As my internship at Mix 103 Radio draws to a close, please know that working here has been a wonderful experience for me. I am grateful for the training and advice I have received over the past twelve months.

I'd especially like to thank my boss and mentor, Leslie Brighton, from whom I have not only learned the fundamentals of radio advertising, but also how to meet customers' needs. Her nomination for this year's Orlando Trophy speaks volumes about her dedication to her clients and staff.

I also appreciate the video recording you presented to me, showing me at work and at play here. I will miss joining many of you for lunches at the Michele's Pizza. I know that all of you have my contact information, so don't hesitate to stay in touch!

Sincerely,
Casey O'Meara

GO ON TO THE NEXT PAGE.

Orlando Small Business Trophy Winners

Advertising and Social Media Category

Platinum: Leslie Brighton, Advertising, Mix 103 Radio

Gold: Nina Li, Marketing, Davenport Clothing Stores

Silver: Jorge Cortez, Cortez Publicity Company

Bronze: Thom Royce, Social Media Technology, Mix 103 Radio

Winners were selected from over 50 nominations. The recipient of the Platinum Orlando Trophy will be profiled in the December issue of Orlando Business Today. Awards will be presented by the Orlando Business Association at a gala event in the banquet hall of the Peachtree Disney Hotel on October 12.

191. What does Mr. Swinney indicate about Mix 103 Radio?
(A) It resolved his problem adequately.
(B) It is a rapidly growing company.
(C) It advertises local business only.
(D) It charges an extra fee to new clients.

192. What is suggested about Mr. Swinney?
(A) He has been a client of Mix 103 Radio for many years.
(B) He was assisted by an intern at Mix 103 Radio.
(C) He recently experienced a decline in his car sales.
(D) He runs the biggest automotive business in the area.

193. Why did Ms. O'Meara send the e-mail?
(A) To ask for help from co-workers.
(B) To organize a luncheon.
(C) To arrange a video recording session.
(D) To thank staff members.

195. What does the webpage suggest?
(A) The gala event is open to the public.
(B) Fewer awards nominations were received this year.
(C) Mr. Royce and Ms. Brighton are colleagues.
(D) Winners will receive a free subscription to Orlando Business Today.

194. What award will be presented to Ms. O'Meara's supervisor?
(A) Platinum.
(B) Gold.
(C) Silver.
(D) Bronze.

MEMO

To: All Full-Time Staff
Subject: Vacation Days

All full-time staff members must submit requests for leave through the company's Timekeeper website. An authorization e-mail will be sent through Timekeeper after dates are approved by the appropriate supervisor.

Catering Services Department employees: Note that requests for vacation during our peak season (June through September) require additional approval from the General Manager.

Supervisors will coordinate with other members of the department to ensure that all the absent employee's duties will be covered and will inform the Human Resources team how responsibilities have been reassigned.

Requests for time off should be submitted at least three weeks in advance. Human Resources will post a calendar on Timekeeper with all planned vacations, including names of employees assigned to cover those on vacation.

For questions regarding this policy, please contact our Human Resources Department.

Carl Steinberg, Manager

GO ON TO THE NEXT PAGE.

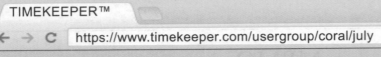

← → C   https://www.timekeeper.com/usergroup/coral/july   ≡

July

PLEASE NOTE: Employees covering for colleagues are responsible for checking the department e-mail account and responding to any time-sensitive messages.

Vacation Dates	Department	Employee	Duties covered by:
1st–5th (Tuesday–Saturday)	Catering Services	Yuki Fukada	Ricky Nix
7th–11th (Monday–Friday)	Guest Services	Carmen de Vera	Oskar Gustafson
18th–20th (Friday–Sunday)	Hospitality	Dieter Sheine	Savannah Quisley
20th–24th (Sunday–Thursday)	Human Resources	Carl Steinberg	Anders Witt

From:	Oliver Champ <ochamp@ep.com>
To:	Carmen de Vera <guestservices@coralembassy.com>
Re:	Reservation BX2523D
Date:	July 7

Dear Ms. de Vera,

We currently have a reservation for one of our executives, Mr. Charles Hodges, for the night of July 8. However, our clients have asked us to reschedule his presentation at their office and therefore we will need to move the reservation to July 11. Would you please confirm that there is a room available for that date?

Thank you for your assistance.

Regards,
Oscar Champ
Administrative Assistant
Pyramid Pharmaceuticals

196. According to the memo, what should an employee do to schedule a vacation?
(A) Send an e-mail to a manager.
(B) Visit a company website.
(C) Contact Human Resources.
(D) Inform a supervisor.

197. In the e-mail, what type of business is Mr. Champ contacting?
(A) A hotel.
(B) A restaurant.
(C) An airline.
(D) A conference center.

198. Who will most likely respond to Mr. Champ's e-mail?
(A) Ms. Steinberg.
(B) Mr. Nix.
(C) Ms. De Vera.
(D) Mr. Gustafson.

199. Which vacation period in the table will require approval by the general manager?
(A) July 18-20.
(B) July 7-11.
(C) July 1-5.
(D) July 20-24.

200. In the table, what is indicated about the employees' company?
(A) It operates seven days a week.
(B) It plans to hire additional staff in July
(C) It requires vacations not to overlap.
(D) It closes some departments in July.

Stop! This is the end of the test. If you finish before time is called, you may go back to Parts 5, 6, and 7 and check your work.

GO ON TO THE NEXT PAGE.

NO TEST MATERIAL ON THIS PAGE

New TOEIC Listening Script

PART 1

1. (　　) (A) This is a baseball stadium.
   (B) This is a textile factory.
   (C) This is a swimming pool.
   (D) This is an ice-skating rink.

2. (　　) (A) She is a street vendor.
   (B) She is a police officer.
   (C) She is a teacher.
   (D) She is a clerk.

3. (　　) (A) The girl is near the tree.
   (B) Several birds are in the water.
   (C) The girl is wearing a coat.
   (D) This is an aquarium.

4. (　　) (A) They are fighting.
   (B) They are sewing.
   (C) They are dancing.
   (D) They are farming.

5. (　　) (A) This is an office building.
   (B) This is a public park.
   (C) This is a shopping mall.
   (D) This is a private home.

6. (　　) (A) They are woodworking.
   (B) They are cooking.
   (C) They are landscaping.
   (D) They are painting.

GO ON TO THE NEXT PAGE.

PART 2

7. (   ) Who made the decision to cancel the program?
   (A) Not me.
   (B) That was my favorite program.
   (C) Make the decision.

8. (   ) Do you mind if I sit here?
   (A) It's self-serving.
   (B) New and improved.
   (C) I don't mind at all.

9. (   ) Did you make it in time to see James?
   (A) It was exciting.
   (B) No, I just missed him.
   (C) On Tuesday.

10. (   ) What's wrong with Vincent?
    (A) He lost his job today.
    (B) Paint.
    (C) Don't bring me flowers. I'm allergic.

11. (   ) Try to be on time from now on, OK?
    (A) What time? How about six?
    (B) That's right. He's the boss.
    (C) I'm sorry. It will never happen again.

12. (   ) Can I ask you a question?
    (A) Of course.
    (B) It's not my question.
    (C) The jury is out.

13. (   ) Will Mary have the TPS reports by Monday?
    (A) The TPS reports.
    (B) She said she would.
    (C) See you on Monday.

14. (   ) What time does your flight leave?
    (A) Leave it up to me.
    (B) Boom goes the dynamite.
    (C) Noon.

15. (   ) Do you have any plans this weekend?
     (A) Michigan.
     (B) We get paid by the hour.
     (C) I'm going camping with some friends.

16. (   ) Did John make a speech at the meeting?
     (A) Everyone was talking at once.
     (B) There were five people.
     (C) No, Steve did all the talking.

17. (   ) I think we're lost.
     (A) We have a winning record.
     (B) Let's ask someone for directions.
     (C) Alas, poor Yorick.

18. (   ) Why did you get fired from your job?
     (A) I got fired yesterday.
     (B) It's a long story.
     (C) I'm doing the work of two people.

19. (   ) Have you found a replacement for Martha?
     (A) He was a man of infinite jest.
     (B) Not yet.
     (C) Martha is leaving.

20. (   ) How was your date with Henry last night?
     (A) It was nice.
     (B) I saw Henry last night.
     (C) It's the tenth.

21. (   ) You have health insurance, don't you?
     (A) How about if I guarantee it?
     (B) Crumbs.
     (C) No, I can't afford it.

22. (   ) Where can I find a stapler?
     (A) Look in the supply cabinet.
     (B) Put the stapler on my desk.
     (C) I stapled them together.

GO ON TO THE NEXT PAGE.

23. (   ) That's Mr. Brown's car, isn't it?
    (A) Oh, I don't drive.
    (B) Mr. Brown.
    (C) No, that's a Lexus. Mr. Brown drives a BMW.

24. (   ) Do you know how to ski?
    (A) I don't have a dog.
    (B) No, I've never been skiing.
    (C) Yes, you will get the hang of it.

25. (   ) Have you started writing the proposal?
    (A) The job starts tomorrow.
    (B) No, I wasn't able to take it.
    (C) Yes, it will be finished this afternoon.

26. (   ) Why are there police in front of the building?
    (A) Someone must have called them.
    (B) More often than not.
    (C) Four, counting me.

27. (   ) Stop shouting. I'm sitting right here.
    (A) Sorry, I'll try to keep my voice down.
    (B) Sit by the window.
    (C) The man shouted at me.

28. (   ) How long did it take you to get here?
    (A) It should be here soon.
    (B) I've been here since Monday.
    (C) About an hour.

29. (   ) What time do you close?
    (A) I'm very close with him.
    (B) No, he didn't.
    (C) We close at five p.m.

30. (   ) Has today's mail been sent out yet?
    (A) Let me think.
    (B) Yes, it has.
    (C) It was cancelled.

31. (　　) Are those your shoes?
      (A) Adidas.
      (B) Yes, they are.
      (C) I'm wearing shoes.

PART 3

**Questions 32 through 34** refer to the following conversation between three speakers.

M : Excuse me, are you the manager?
Woman UK : Yes. Is there a problem, sir?

M : I ordered the meat loaf special. My server Tiffany said it would be out several times, but I'm obviously still waiting.
Woman UK : About how long ago did you place your order, sir?

M : At least 25 minutes.
Woman UK : Oh, that's unreasonable. Let me find out what the holdup is. Tiffany, this diner has been waiting nearly half an hour for his meal.

Woman US : I'm very sorry, Ms. Reagan. I've asked the chef, but the kitchen is really slow tonight. Two of the line cooks are out sick. Maybe you could step in and make things happen for this gentleman?
Woman UK : Right. Thanks, Tiffany. Sir, I'll ask the chef to send out your meal right away.

32. (　　) Who most likely is Ms. Reagan?
      (A) A travel agent.
      (B) A bank clerk.
      (C) A warehouse supervisor.
      (D) A restaurant manager.

33. (　　) What is the man complaining about?
      (A) An order has not arrived.
      (B) A bill is not accurate.
      (C) An item has been discontinued.
      (D) A reservation was lost.

34. (　　) What does the manager say she will do?
      (A) Delete an account.
      (B) Speak to an employee.
      (C) Refund a purchase.
      (D) Confirm an address.

GO ON TO THE NEXT PAGE.

Questions 35 through 37 *refer to the following conversation.*

M : I'll have a bagel with cream cheese and a small iced coffee.

W : What type of bagel would you prefer? We have poppy seed, onion, and plain.

M : The poppy seed sounds good. And give me extra cream cheese. Oh, but not too much sugar in the coffee.

W : We don't add sugar to your coffee, sir. It's self-serve. You can add sugar at the condiment station to your left.

35. (   ) Who are the speakers?
    (A) Teacher and student.
    (B) Employee and customer.
    (C) Doctor and patient.
    (D) Friend and foe.

36. (   ) Where is this conversation most likely taking place?
    (A) In an office.
    (B) In a cafeteria.
    (C) On a bus.
    (D) At a business meeting.

37. (   ) What does the man ask for?
    (A) An onion bagel.
    (B) Extra sugar in the coffee.
    (C) Extra cream cheese on the bagel.
    (D) Hot coffee.

Questions 38 through 40 *refer to the following conversation.*

M : Mary, did you contact technical support about my computer yet? You know I'm working on the Cooper presentation and all my work is on that hard drive.

W : I called them yesterday, Rex. They said they'd have a guy out here tomorrow afternoon.

M : Tomorrow afternoon? Oh, no, no, no, Mary. That's not going to work! I'm meeting with Cooper and his associates at three o'clock tomorrow afternoon. This is our most important account. I need you to get someone out here today—*today*—no excuses, spare no expense.

W : OK, Rex. I'll try my best.

M : Don't try. Just do it. If the tech support people won't come, call an independent repairman. I don't care who you have to call. I want that computer fixed today.

38. (   ) What is the man's problem?
     (A) His schedule is too full.
     (B) His computer isn't working.
     (C) His confidence is shattered.
     (D) His secretary is on vacation.

39. (   ) What will the man do tomorrow at three o'clock?
     (A) Buy a new computer.
     (B) Meet with a client.
     (C) Leave for a business trip.
     (D) Contact customer service.

40. (   ) What will Mary most likely do next?
     (A) Find someone to fix Rex's computer.
     (B) Cancel the meeting with Cooper.
     (C) Meet with Cooper and his associates.
     (D) Fix Rex's computer herself.

Questions 41 through 43 *refer to the following conversation.*

W : Hi, James! I'm so happy to see you. I need your help. The ATM took my debit card. What should I do?

M : Where did it happen? Was it at the bank or somewhere else?

W : I used an ATM at the shopping mall.

M : OK, well, there should be a phone number to call for these situations. Let's go and check the ATM at the mall.

W: OK, I'll drive.

41. (   ) What is the woman's problem?
     (A) She lost her driver's license.
     (B) She lost her wallet.
     (C) She lost her cell phone.
     (D) She lost her ATM card.

42. (   ) What does the man ask?
     (A) Where it happened.
     (B) How it happened.
     (C) When it happened.
     (D) Why it happened.

GO ON TO THE NEXT PAGE.

43. (　　) What will the speakers most likely do next?
      (A) Make a phone call.
      (B) Drive to the shopping mall.
      (C) Walk to the bank.
      (D) Try another ATM.

Questions 44 through 46 *refer to the following conversation.*

M : Skipping lunch again, Wanda?

W : (Makes hissing sound) Lunch? What's that?

M : I heard your boss is on the war path. He's got everybody in accounting on high alert, too.

W : You guys in marketing have no idea what it's like to work for that man. I'm afraid to leave my desk even to use the bathroom, just in case he comes charging in here looking for God knows what.

44. (　　) What are the speakers discussing?
      (A) Lunch.
      (B) The woman's boss.
      (C) Former clients.
      (D) A shortcut to the cafeteria.

45. (　　) What does the woman imply?
      (A) She's not hungry.
      (B) She's already had lunch.
      (C) She's unable to leave her desk.
      (D) She's happy with her job.

46. (　　) Where does the man work?
      (A) In sales.
      (B) In marketing.
      (C) In accounting.
      (D) In tech support.

Questions 47 through 49 *refer to the following conversation.*

W : That was a great performance, Norman. Where did you learn to play like that?

M : Where or when? My family moved around a lot, so it's not like I was ever in one place for very long. I've been playing since I was four.

W : I mean, did you take lessons or go to a special school?

M : Oh, I see. Neither, actually. I'm completely self-taught. I basically learned by playing along to the radio.

47. (   ) What did Norman do?
        (A) He moved around on stage.
        (B) He grew up quickly.
        (C) He gave a performance.
        (D) He left too soon.

48. (   ) What does the woman ask?
        (A) Where did Norman learn his skill?
        (B) Where did Norman grow up?
        (C) When did Norman take lessons?
        (D) What was Norman's family like?

49. (   ) What is implied about Norman?
        (A) He's arrogant.
        (B) He's a musician.
        (C) He's from a foreign country.
        (D) He's ashamed of his skill.

Questions 50 through 52 refer to the following conversation with three speakers.

M : Hi, Evelyn. I'd like you to meet our new public relations officer, Caroline Wright.
Woman UK : It's nice to meet you, Caroline. Welcome to the firm.

Woman US : Thanks. It's nice to meet you, too.
M : She'll meet the rest of the PR team later today. But I wanted to introduce you now since I believe you live pretty close to each other. Evelyn, I know you were looking for someone to share rides with.

Woman UK : Yes! Caroline, where do you live?
Woman US : Near Sunset Avenue and Carver Street, in West Palmdale.

Woman UK : Oh! I'm at Hollywood and Carver! That's so close! Would you be interested in carpooling together?
Woman US : Sure! That would be great. Can I get your phone number so that we can discuss it later today?

50. (   ) In which department do the speakers work?
        (A) Accounting.
        (B) Public Relations.
        (C) Human Resources.
        (D) Marketing.

GO ON TO THE NEXT PAGE.

51. (   ) What does Caroline Wright ask for?
        (A) An instruction manual.
        (B) A password.
        (C) Some survey results.
        (D) A telephone number.

52. (   ) What does the man suggest that the women do?
        (A) Organize an event.
        (B) Drive to work together.
        (C) Share a workspace.
        (D) Submit a resume.

Questions 53 through 55 *refer to the following conversation.*

W : Did you get my e-mail?

M : Yes, obviously. That's why I'm here. What did you need to see me about?

W : Apparently, there's a rumor going around that Ben is going to leave the company. Do you know anything about it?

M : This is the first time I'm hearing of it. What makes you think I might have any information? I'm just a lowly mail clerk.

53. (   ) What are the speakers discussing?
        (A) Company gossip.
        (B) Study habits.
        (C) Political theory.
        (D) Vacation time.

54. (   ) What does the woman ask the man?
        (A) If he plans on leaving the company.
        (B) If he has spoken to Ben recently.
        (C) If he knows anything about a rumor.
        (D) If he wants to have lunch.

55. (   ) What does the man imply?
        (A) He has low status within the company.
        (B) He doesn't pay attention to gossip.
        (C) He has a close relationship with Ben.
        (D) He might be the source of the rumor.

W : Hi. That's my Honda out there. It's, um, making a really strange noise.

M : Can you describe the noise? Where is the noise coming from?

W : Well, it sounds like metal rubbing on metal, or something grinding against something metal. I think it's coming from the engine. I don't know anything about cars. The noise is really horrible.

M : OK, well, let's have a look under the hood.

56. (   ) Where is this conversation taking place?
    (A) At an auto repair shop.
    (B) At a discount grocery.
    (C) At a metal processing factory.
    (D) At a busy intersection.

57. (   ) What kind of problem does the woman have?
    (A) Auto-immune.
    (B) Auto-pilot.
    (C) Automotive.
    (D) Automatic.

58. (   ) What will the speakers most likely do next?
    (A) Sign a contract.
    (B) Inspect the woman's car.
    (C) Shake hands and call it a deal.
    (D) Watch a video about automobile maintenance.

Questions 59 through 61 *refer to the following conversation.*

W : Did you hear that Bill Rubin is being transferred to headquarters in Oslo?

M : Really? That's a shocker. He's been killing it here, especially since he came back from Shanghai with all those Chinese accounts. Did you know he single-handedly doubled our revenue in London?

W : Well, that's probably why he's taking over for Brent Hines as director of European operations. Their numbers are in the tank. They need a superstar like Rubin to save the sinking ship.

M : Well, good for Bill. But I've got to say, I'd rather go anyplace other than Norway in the dead of winter.

GO ON TO THE NEXT PAGE.

59. (   ) Why is Bill Rubin being transferred to Oslo?
    (A) To become director of European operations.
    (B) To placate Chinese investors.
    (C) To increase sales in London.
    (D) To assist Brent Hines.

60. (   ) Where did Bill Rubin double revenues?
    (A) Shanghai.
    (B) London.
    (C) Oslo.
    (D) Paris.

61. (   ) What does the man imply?
    (A) Norway is extremely cold in winter.
    (B) Shanghai would have been a better fit.
    (C) London won't miss him.
    (D) Oslo is flooded.

Questions 62 through 64 refer to the following conversation.

W : Best Western Gateway, front desk, this is Amy speaking. How may I direct your call?

M : Um, yeah, I was trying to get in touch with the front desk. I'm in room 303...

W : Sir, this is the front desk. How can I help you?

M : Oh, right. Well, you see, this is kind of embarrassing but I can't seem to figure out how the television works. I mean, it's *on*, but all I get is a blank blue screen.

W : Room 303? OK, sir. I'll send housekeeping up there right away to resolve your issue. Is there anything else I can do for you?

62. (   ) Where are the speakers?
    (A) In school.
    (B) On a television set.
    (C) In a hotel.
    (D) On a journey.

63. (   ) What is the man's problem?
    (A) His room is too cold.
    (B) He would like to order room service.
    (C) The television isn't working.
    (D) The walls are too thin.

64. (   ) What does the woman say she will do?
  (A) Replace the television in the man's room.
  (B) Send someone to solve the man's problem.
  (C) Reset the cable television system.
  (D) Move the man to a different room.

Questions 65 through 67 _refer to the following conversation with three speakers._

Woman UK : I've called this meeting to get an update on our company's new restaurant finder smart phone application. We're due to start consumer testing of the app next month. Darren, you're the lead developer. Why don't you bring us up to date?

M : Unfortunately, we've had some bugs in the app software. That's why I asked Meredith to join us. She's in charge of software development.

Woman UK : Meredith, what can you tell me?

Woman US : Well, we've run into some unexpected problems with a feature that tracks the users' current location. We're hoping to get it fixed shortly.

Woman UK : This is an important product for our company. So, Darren, please send me a thorough update by the end of the day tomorrow.

M : Absolutely, Ms. Barrymore. As soon as possible.

65. (   ) What are the speakers talking about?
  (A) A smart phone application.
  (B) Computer tablets.
  (C) Music players.
  (D) Digital cameras.

66. (   ) What problem does the man mention?
  (A) Customer testing has been delayed.
  (B) Costs have been higher than estimated.
  (C) There has been a shortage of parts.
  (D) Some software is not working properly.

67. (   ) What does the man mean by //"Absolutely, Ms. Barrymore."//?
  (A) He will provide a report.
  (B) He will hire more programmers.
  (C) He believes the problem has been resolved.
  (D) He accepts responsibility for the mistake.

GO ON TO THE NEXT PAGE.

M : Did you notice the light is burned out in the hallway closet?

W : Yes, I did. I was going to ask you to change it.

M : No problem. Do we have any spare bulbs?

W : We do. I picked up a couple of those new energy-saving bulbs from the hardware store.

68. (   ) What does the man ask the woman?
    (A) If she wants him to change the light in the hallway closet.
    (B) If she reorganized the hallway closet.
    (C) If she is planning on changing the light in the hallway closet.
    (D) If she noticed the light is burned out in the hallway closet.

69. (   ) What does the woman say?
    (A) That she didn't notice the light is out.
    (B) That she was going to ask the man to change it.
    (C) That she is going out to buy light bulbs.
    (D) That she is concerned about saving energy.

70. (   ) What will the man most likely do next?
    (A) Change the light bulb in the hallway closet.
    (B) Go down to the hardware store.
    (C) Ask the woman to change the light bulb in the hallway closet.
    (D) Change all the light bulbs in the house.

PART 4

Questions 71 through 73 *refer to the excerpt from an introduction.*

Welcome to Center Park. Today we're proud to unveil this life-size statue of our city founder, William Center. The funding for this project was courtesy of a donation from the Center City Culture Foundation, and the statue was sculpted by a local artist, Mr. Kurt Black. We are honored to have Mr. Black with us this morning. Kurt is a native of Center City and he comes from a family of artists, many of whom graduated from the New York Institute of Art. He has been sculpting statues since he was 16 and his work is displayed in museums all over the world, as well. Today Kurt will tell you about carving this statue from an old portrait of William Center, a process which took several months. Please join me in welcoming Mr. Kurt Black.

71. (   ) What is true about Kurt Black?
    (A) He founded Center City.
    (B) His paintings are famous all over the world.
    (C) He comes from a family of artists.
    (D) His statue of William Center was self-financed.

72. (   ) What will Kurt Black talk about?
    (A) William Center.
    (B) The carving of the statue.
    (C) Portrait photography.
    (D) New York Institute of Art.

73. (   ) Who paid for the project?
    (A) William Center.
    (B) The Center City Cultural Foundation.
    (C) Kurt Black.
    (D) The New York Institute of Art.

Questions 74 through 76 are based on the following talk.

Obviously, your dishwasher is convenient. But did you also know that it's one of your best allies in keeping your kitchen safe from contaminants? The dishwasher sanitizes everything that goes in it, *if* you use the dry cycle. During that cycle, the internal temperature of the dishwasher reaches 170°F, which is required for sanitizing—the process of reducing harmful microbes to an acceptable level. Of course, sterilizing is something we can't aspire to in our own homes. However, you should always run anything through the dishwasher that can go into it, including glassware, flatware, plates, plastic cutting boards, and sponges. Anything that touches raw meat and fish, or their juices or blood, should be placed in the dishwasher immediately. That means if you use a sponge to wipe up the counter that's been in contact with raw meat, you should toss it right in the dishwasher and get out a clean one. At the very least, your sponges should go into the dishwasher every time you run it. Be sure to keep a backup supply on hand so you are not tempted to use a dirty one.

GO ON TO THE NEXT PAGE.

74. (　) What is the main purpose of this talk?
    (A) To inform.
    (B) To accuse.
    (C) To sell.
    (D) To oppose.

75. (　) What does the speaker suggest?
    (A) Washing hands frequently.
    (B) Using cold water.
    (C) Using the dry cycle of the dishwasher.
    (D) Sterilizing all food used in the kitchen.

76. (　) What is required for sanitizing?
    (A) Raw meat or fish.
    (B) 170°F.
    (C) Glassware.
    (D) Sponges.

Questions 77 through 79 _refer to the following excerpt from a seminar._

How do we attract and retain customers? For a retail superstore like Massive Mart, it's probably the most important question to address. First, we pay a great deal of attention to detail—the store's immediate physical appearance, the lighting, and especially the cleanliness. Cleanliness is a big thing for me, since it's the first thing I look for when I go somewhere. Is the parking lot clean? Are the signs visible and easy to read? Second, we invest in our employees. The benefits package is great. We pay generous salaries, we pay monthly bonuses, and we offer a structured retirement plan. We believe that satisfied workers equal satisfied customers. We just introduced something we call All Hands On Deck. In the busiest hours, from 4 p.m. to 8 p.m., we stop all activity that the customers can't see, like back room unloading and organizing, and put every salesclerk and cashier out on the floor. It's really that hands-on experience that makes people want to come back. We hear from about 50,000 customers each week, and they rate us on a number of attributes. So far, they tell us that we're doing the right thing.

77. (   ) Who is most likely the speaker?
    (A) A corporate manager.
    (B) A sales clerk.
    (C) A cashier.
    (D) A parking lot attendant.

78. (   ) What is the speaker talking about?
    (A) A shipping company.
    (B) A parking garage.
    (C) A marketing agency.
    (D) A retail store.

79. (   ) Which of the following is NOT an employee benefit?
    (A) Generous salaries.
    (B) Monthly bonuses.
    (C) A retirement plan.
    (D) Free parking.

Questions 80 through 82 *refer to the following news report.*

This is Coralynn Guest with a KBUT news update. We have some spectacular video footage of firefighters working to contain the forest fire at Mount Holyoke. As you can see, the inferno continues to rage out of control. A spokesman for the Mount Holyoke Forest Reserve estimates that 30% of the fire is under containment. Investigators have not yet determined the cause of the fire, which has already caused an estimated $500 million in damage to homes in the Mount Holyoke area. There is good news for the fire crews as Mother Nature will provide some relief. A look at the KBUT weather map shows a storm front headed our way this afternoon and evening, expected to bring heavy rain and thundershowers. The skies should begin to clear up tomorrow evening, and the wind will die down, giving those firefighters a break. Meanwhile, the weekend is expected to be clear and dry. In other news, the financial markets are volatile at this hour after hitting a morning low, followed by a tremendous buying surge that set record highs on both the NASDAQ and Dow Jones. Finally, in sports, the Dodgers lost to the Reds 3-2 in extra innings last night and have tonight off before hosting Seattle tomorrow. I'm Coralynn Guest for KBUT news.

GO ON TO THE NEXT PAGE.

80. (   ) Where was this report most likely being broadcast?
    (A) Radio.
    (B) Internet.
    (C) Television.
    (D) Public Address system.

81. (   ) What happened at Mount Holyoke?
    (A) A baseball game.
    (B) A forest fire.
    (C) A thunderstorm.
    (D) A traffic jam.

82. (   ) What will most likely happen tonight?
    (A) The Dodgers will go to Seattle.
    (B) The fire will be contained.
    (C) The skies will clear up.
    (D) The storm front will bring rain.

Questions 83 through 85 _refer to the following announcement._

This is Oliver Hamilton, director of Tulsa Community Services and I'm pleased to announce our annual collection of charity items. Trucks will be deployed across the city next Tuesday, the 15th. We're looking for donations of clean used clothing, cookware, household utensils, and books and games in good condition. We cannot accept computers or large appliances. We ask that you place donated items on your front porch or the curb in front of your house. Set them out by seven in the morning on the 15th, and mark them "CS" in large letters. We will pick them up sometime before five p.m. If you have any questions or want to schedule a pickup for a different date, please call 800-456-1122 between eight a.m. and five p.m. Monday through Friday. Thank you, and have a great day.

83. (   ) What is the main purpose of this announcement?
    (A) To promote a business.
    (B) To solicit charity donations.
    (C) To explain a policy.
    (D) To remind someone of an appointment.

84. (   ) When are the trucks scheduled to be deployed?
  (A) Monday through Friday.
  (B) Anytime before five p.m.
  (C) On Tuesday the 15th.
  (D) Throughout the month.

85. (   ) What is not accepted?
  (A) Household utensils.
  (B) Large appliances.
  (C) Used clothing.
  (D) Cookware.

Questions 86 through 88 *refer to the following talk.*

In my opinion, investments are based on your tolerance for risk. In other words, not just how much money can you stand to lose, but how much are you willing to lose? The stock market is clearly the fast track to success. The upside of investing in stocks is that you can profit in a short time, but it's also a risk. You could get killed in the stock market faster than you can say, "Chapter 11." I've made and lost so many fortunes in the stock market that I've lost track. Therefore, I personally wouldn't invest in stocks with money I figure I'm going to need in the next five years. Bonds have less risk than stocks, but the downside is that the return is small and slow in coming. You know, folks, it may sound like some kind of folksy, down-home wisdom but I measure the safety of my investments by how much sleep I lose worrying about them. Let me give you an example of an investment that kept me awake all night.

86. (   ) Who is the speaker most likely to be?
  (A) A successful investment broker.
  (B) A sleep therapist.
  (C) An author of folk tales.
  (D) A serial killer.

87. (   ) What does the speaker say about the stock market?
  (A) It is lethal.
  (B) It is risky.
  (C) It is sleepy.
  (D) It is folksy.

GO ON TO THE NEXT PAGE.

88. (   ) How does the speaker measure the risk of his investments?
     (A) By hand.
     (B) By how much money he makes or loses.
     (C) By keeping track of his fortunes.
     (D) By how much sleep he loses worrying about them.

Questions 89 through 91 *refer to the following introduction.*

OK, now it's time for the highlight of the evening. My name's Ralph Baker, and I'm the emcee for tonight's program. It's my privilege to introduce our featured speaker, Mr. Phil Spitz. Ten years ago, Phil started brewing beer that was based on his grandfather Ben's recipe. If you haven't heard of Ben's Beer yet, you soon will. Last year Mr. Spitz signed a distribution agreement with a national distributor, and soon Ben's Beer will be a household name. Tonight Phil, who's only 26, will discuss what it's like to be a successful entrepreneur at such a young age, and where he will take his young company from here. Mr. Spitz will speak for about 60 minutes. Please save all your questions for the end of his speech, when there will be a 30-minute question-and-answer session. If you have a question for Phil at that time, raise your hand, and one of our ushers will bring you a wireless microphone so that everyone in the room will be able to hear you. So without further ado, please welcome Mr. Phil Spitz.

89. (   ) Who is being introduced?
     (A) An elderly beer maker.
     (B) A famous politician.
     (C) A corporate executive.
     (D) A young entrepreneur.

90. (   ) What will the speaker talk about?
     (A) His education.
     (B) His business.
     (C) His religion.
     (D) His family.

91. (   ) When can the audience ask questions?
     (A) At the end of the speech.
     (B) Before the speech begins.
     (C) 30 minutes later.
     (D) There will be no questions allowed.

May I have your attention, please? Bus 7-1-8 from Denver, scheduled to arrive at 10:57, is experiencing mechanical difficulties and is currently stalled just outside the city limits. A new bus is en route to transport passengers and is expected to be here in about an hour. We apologize for the delay. Meanwhile, passengers waiting for bus 7-1-8 to Las Vegas and Los Angeles are invited to have a free meal in our lounge. Show your boarding pass at the dining counter to receive lunch and a beverage, on us. If you are a 7-1-8 passenger planning to catch connecting buses in Las Vegas or Los Angeles, we are phoning those stations and trying to arrange for extra buses to meet you and avoid further delays. We apologize again for this inconvenience. Please note that our on-time rate is better than 90 percent. If you would like a refund due to this postponement, please take your boarding pass to the customer service desk in the back of the station.

92. (   ) Where does this announcement take place?
     (A) On the radio.
     (B) At a business meeting.
     (C) On television.
     (D) In a bus station.

93. (   ) What caused the 7-1-8 bus to be late?
     (A) A snow storm in Denver.
     (B) Heavy traffic in Los Angeles.
     (C) Mechanical trouble on the outskirts of the city.
     (D) Parades in Las Vegas.

94. (   ) What should listeners do if they want a refund?
     (A) Take the 7-1-8 bus to Las Vegas.
     (B) Bring their boarding passes to customer service.
     (C) Have lunch in the lounge.
     (D) Complain to the manager.

GO ON TO THE NEXT PAGE.

It's June and that means Buffalo Jed's Furniture is hosting its annual summer sale, and right now our very popular dining room table is on sale for 75% off the original price! This deal is valid for in-store purchases only. You can just pick it up from the store. All of the parts are included in one small box. Our customers love this dining room table because it can be assembled at home quickly and easily. Just log on to our website to access our simple assembly instructions. Don't miss out on this deal! Come visit us at Buffalo Jed's Furniture today, where the prices just couldn't get any lower.

95. (   ) Look at the graphic. What is the sale price of the table being described?
    (A) $18.00.
    (B) $25.00.
    (C) $27.50.
    (D) $30.00.

Item	Original Price	Sale Price
Dining room table	$100.00	$25.00
Coffee table	$54.00	$18.00
Patio table	$90.00	$30.00
Kitchen table	$110.00	$27.50

96. (   ) According to the speaker, why do customers like the table?
    (A) It is hand-made.
    (B) It is available in many colors.
    (C) It is easy to assemble.
    (D) It is inexpensive.

97. (   ) What does the speaker say can be found on a website?
    (A) Some instructions.
    (B) Some recipes.
    (C) A warranty.
    (D) A coupon.

Hey Lindsey, this is Dylan. I'm calling about the music festival we've been planning to help raise funds for breast cancer awareness. Got a problem here, Lindsey. Have you seen the weather forecast? Apparently, it's supposed to be unseasonably hot on the day we were planning to hold our event. Over 102 degrees. Even with the use of industrial fans on stage, none of the performers will want to play under those conditions. So, I'd like you to get the team together tomorrow sometime to get things in order for an alternate date. Could you organize that? Mostly minor planning adjustments that we'll need to make.

98. (   ) What event is being discussed?
    (A) A grand opening.
    (B) A charity walk.
    (C) A trip to the zoo.
    (D) A music festival.

99. (   ) Look at the graphic. Which day was the event originally scheduled for?
    (A) Thursday.
    (B) Friday.
    (C) Saturday.
    (D) Sunday.

CHARLOTTESVILLE WEEKEND WEATHER FORECAST			
Thursday	Friday	Saturday	Sunday
Cloudy and humid	Partly cloudy with scattered thunderstorms	Extreme heat advisory	Sunny with onshore winds
Hi: 95 / Lo: 78	Hi: 97 / Lo: 83	Hi: 103 / Lo: 88	Hi: 96 / Lo: 80

100. (   ) What does the speaker ask the listener to do?
    (A) Arrange a meeting.
    (B) Contact scheduled performers.
    (C) Rent industrial fans.
    (D) Print new tickets.

NO TEST MATERIAL ON THIS PAGE

TOEIC ANSWER SHEET

REGISTRATION No.

姓 名
N A M E

LISTENING SECTION

Part 1

No.	ANSWER A B C D
1	Ⓐ Ⓑ Ⓒ Ⓓ
2	Ⓐ Ⓑ Ⓒ Ⓓ
3	Ⓐ Ⓑ Ⓒ Ⓓ
4	Ⓐ Ⓑ Ⓒ Ⓓ
5	Ⓐ Ⓑ Ⓒ Ⓓ
6	Ⓐ Ⓑ Ⓒ Ⓓ
7	Ⓐ Ⓑ Ⓒ
8	Ⓐ Ⓑ Ⓒ
9	Ⓐ Ⓑ Ⓒ
10	Ⓐ Ⓑ Ⓒ

Part 2

No.	ANSWER A B C
11	Ⓐ Ⓑ Ⓒ
12	Ⓐ Ⓑ Ⓒ
13	Ⓐ Ⓑ Ⓒ
14	Ⓐ Ⓑ Ⓒ
15	Ⓐ Ⓑ Ⓒ
16	Ⓐ Ⓑ Ⓒ
17	Ⓐ Ⓑ Ⓒ
18	Ⓐ Ⓑ Ⓒ
19	Ⓐ Ⓑ Ⓒ
20	Ⓐ Ⓑ Ⓒ

No.	ANSWER A B C
21	Ⓐ Ⓑ Ⓒ
22	Ⓐ Ⓑ Ⓒ
23	Ⓐ Ⓑ Ⓒ
24	Ⓐ Ⓑ Ⓒ
25	Ⓐ Ⓑ Ⓒ
26	Ⓐ Ⓑ Ⓒ
27	Ⓐ Ⓑ Ⓒ
28	Ⓐ Ⓑ Ⓒ
29	Ⓐ Ⓑ Ⓒ
30	Ⓐ Ⓑ Ⓒ

Part 3

No.	ANSWER A B C D
31	Ⓐ Ⓑ Ⓒ
32	Ⓐ Ⓑ Ⓒ Ⓓ
33	Ⓐ Ⓑ Ⓒ Ⓓ
34	Ⓐ Ⓑ Ⓒ Ⓓ
35	Ⓐ Ⓑ Ⓒ Ⓓ
36	Ⓐ Ⓑ Ⓒ Ⓓ
37	Ⓐ Ⓑ Ⓒ Ⓓ
38	Ⓐ Ⓑ Ⓒ Ⓓ
39	Ⓐ Ⓑ Ⓒ Ⓓ
40	Ⓐ Ⓑ Ⓒ Ⓓ

No.	ANSWER A B C D
41	Ⓐ Ⓑ Ⓒ Ⓓ
42	Ⓐ Ⓑ Ⓒ Ⓓ
43	Ⓐ Ⓑ Ⓒ Ⓓ
44	Ⓐ Ⓑ Ⓒ Ⓓ
45	Ⓐ Ⓑ Ⓒ Ⓓ
46	Ⓐ Ⓑ Ⓒ Ⓓ
47	Ⓐ Ⓑ Ⓒ Ⓓ
48	Ⓐ Ⓑ Ⓒ Ⓓ
49	Ⓐ Ⓑ Ⓒ Ⓓ
50	Ⓐ Ⓑ Ⓒ Ⓓ

No.	ANSWER A B C D
51	Ⓐ Ⓑ Ⓒ Ⓓ
52	Ⓐ Ⓑ Ⓒ Ⓓ
53	Ⓐ Ⓑ Ⓒ Ⓓ
54	Ⓐ Ⓑ Ⓒ Ⓓ
55	Ⓐ Ⓑ Ⓒ Ⓓ
56	Ⓐ Ⓑ Ⓒ Ⓓ
57	Ⓐ Ⓑ Ⓒ Ⓓ
58	Ⓐ Ⓑ Ⓒ Ⓓ
59	Ⓐ Ⓑ Ⓒ Ⓓ
60	Ⓐ Ⓑ Ⓒ Ⓓ

Part 4

No.	ANSWER A B C D
61	Ⓐ Ⓑ Ⓒ Ⓓ
62	Ⓐ Ⓑ Ⓒ Ⓓ
63	Ⓐ Ⓑ Ⓒ Ⓓ
64	Ⓐ Ⓑ Ⓒ Ⓓ
65	Ⓐ Ⓑ Ⓒ Ⓓ
66	Ⓐ Ⓑ Ⓒ Ⓓ
67	Ⓐ Ⓑ Ⓒ Ⓓ
68	Ⓐ Ⓑ Ⓒ Ⓓ
69	Ⓐ Ⓑ Ⓒ Ⓓ
70	Ⓐ Ⓑ Ⓒ Ⓓ

No.	ANSWER A B C D
71	Ⓐ Ⓑ Ⓒ Ⓓ
72	Ⓐ Ⓑ Ⓒ Ⓓ
73	Ⓐ Ⓑ Ⓒ Ⓓ
74	Ⓐ Ⓑ Ⓒ Ⓓ
75	Ⓐ Ⓑ Ⓒ Ⓓ
76	Ⓐ Ⓑ Ⓒ Ⓓ
77	Ⓐ Ⓑ Ⓒ Ⓓ
78	Ⓐ Ⓑ Ⓒ Ⓓ
79	Ⓐ Ⓑ Ⓒ Ⓓ
80	Ⓐ Ⓑ Ⓒ Ⓓ

No.	ANSWER A B C D
81	Ⓐ Ⓑ Ⓒ Ⓓ
82	Ⓐ Ⓑ Ⓒ Ⓓ
83	Ⓐ Ⓑ Ⓒ Ⓓ
84	Ⓐ Ⓑ Ⓒ Ⓓ
85	Ⓐ Ⓑ Ⓒ Ⓓ
86	Ⓐ Ⓑ Ⓒ Ⓓ
87	Ⓐ Ⓑ Ⓒ Ⓓ
88	Ⓐ Ⓑ Ⓒ Ⓓ
89	Ⓐ Ⓑ Ⓒ Ⓓ
90	Ⓐ Ⓑ Ⓒ Ⓓ

No.	ANSWER A B C D
91	Ⓐ Ⓑ Ⓒ Ⓓ
92	Ⓐ Ⓑ Ⓒ Ⓓ
93	Ⓐ Ⓑ Ⓒ Ⓓ
94	Ⓐ Ⓑ Ⓒ Ⓓ
95	Ⓐ Ⓑ Ⓒ Ⓓ
96	Ⓐ Ⓑ Ⓒ Ⓓ
97	Ⓐ Ⓑ Ⓒ Ⓓ
98	Ⓐ Ⓑ Ⓒ Ⓓ
99	Ⓐ Ⓑ Ⓒ Ⓓ
100	Ⓐ Ⓑ Ⓒ Ⓓ

READING SECTION

Part 5

No.	ANSWER A B C D
101	Ⓐ Ⓑ Ⓒ Ⓓ
102	Ⓐ Ⓑ Ⓒ Ⓓ
103	Ⓐ Ⓑ Ⓒ Ⓓ
104	Ⓐ Ⓑ Ⓒ Ⓓ
105	Ⓐ Ⓑ Ⓒ Ⓓ
106	Ⓐ Ⓑ Ⓒ Ⓓ
107	Ⓐ Ⓑ Ⓒ Ⓓ
108	Ⓐ Ⓑ Ⓒ Ⓓ
109	Ⓐ Ⓑ Ⓒ Ⓓ
110	Ⓐ Ⓑ Ⓒ Ⓓ

No.	ANSWER A B C D
111	Ⓐ Ⓑ Ⓒ Ⓓ
112	Ⓐ Ⓑ Ⓒ Ⓓ
113	Ⓐ Ⓑ Ⓒ Ⓓ
114	Ⓐ Ⓑ Ⓒ Ⓓ
115	Ⓐ Ⓑ Ⓒ Ⓓ
116	Ⓐ Ⓑ Ⓒ Ⓓ
117	Ⓐ Ⓑ Ⓒ Ⓓ
118	Ⓐ Ⓑ Ⓒ Ⓓ
119	Ⓐ Ⓑ Ⓒ Ⓓ
120	Ⓐ Ⓑ Ⓒ Ⓓ

Part 6

No.	ANSWER A B C D
121	Ⓐ Ⓑ Ⓒ Ⓓ
122	Ⓐ Ⓑ Ⓒ Ⓓ
123	Ⓐ Ⓑ Ⓒ Ⓓ
124	Ⓐ Ⓑ Ⓒ Ⓓ
125	Ⓐ Ⓑ Ⓒ Ⓓ
126	Ⓐ Ⓑ Ⓒ Ⓓ
127	Ⓐ Ⓑ Ⓒ Ⓓ
128	Ⓐ Ⓑ Ⓒ Ⓓ
129	Ⓐ Ⓑ Ⓒ Ⓓ
130	Ⓐ Ⓑ Ⓒ Ⓓ

No.	ANSWER A B C D
131	Ⓐ Ⓑ Ⓒ Ⓓ
132	Ⓐ Ⓑ Ⓒ Ⓓ
133	Ⓐ Ⓑ Ⓒ Ⓓ
134	Ⓐ Ⓑ Ⓒ Ⓓ
135	Ⓐ Ⓑ Ⓒ Ⓓ
136	Ⓐ Ⓑ Ⓒ Ⓓ
137	Ⓐ Ⓑ Ⓒ Ⓓ
138	Ⓐ Ⓑ Ⓒ Ⓓ
139	Ⓐ Ⓑ Ⓒ Ⓓ
140	Ⓐ Ⓑ Ⓒ Ⓓ

Part 7

No.	ANSWER A B C D
141	Ⓐ Ⓑ Ⓒ Ⓓ
142	Ⓐ Ⓑ Ⓒ Ⓓ
143	Ⓐ Ⓑ Ⓒ Ⓓ
144	Ⓐ Ⓑ Ⓒ Ⓓ
145	Ⓐ Ⓑ Ⓒ Ⓓ
146	Ⓐ Ⓑ Ⓒ Ⓓ
147	Ⓐ Ⓑ Ⓒ Ⓓ
148	Ⓐ Ⓑ Ⓒ Ⓓ
149	Ⓐ Ⓑ Ⓒ Ⓓ
150	Ⓐ Ⓑ Ⓒ Ⓓ

No.	ANSWER A B C D
151	Ⓐ Ⓑ Ⓒ Ⓓ
152	Ⓐ Ⓑ Ⓒ Ⓓ
153	Ⓐ Ⓑ Ⓒ Ⓓ
154	Ⓐ Ⓑ Ⓒ Ⓓ
155	Ⓐ Ⓑ Ⓒ Ⓓ
156	Ⓐ Ⓑ Ⓒ Ⓓ
157	Ⓐ Ⓑ Ⓒ Ⓓ
158	Ⓐ Ⓑ Ⓒ Ⓓ
159	Ⓐ Ⓑ Ⓒ Ⓓ
160	Ⓐ Ⓑ Ⓒ Ⓓ

No.	ANSWER A B C D
161	Ⓐ Ⓑ Ⓒ Ⓓ
162	Ⓐ Ⓑ Ⓒ Ⓓ
163	Ⓐ Ⓑ Ⓒ Ⓓ
164	Ⓐ Ⓑ Ⓒ Ⓓ
165	Ⓐ Ⓑ Ⓒ Ⓓ
166	Ⓐ Ⓑ Ⓒ Ⓓ
167	Ⓐ Ⓑ Ⓒ Ⓓ
168	Ⓐ Ⓑ Ⓒ Ⓓ
169	Ⓐ Ⓑ Ⓒ Ⓓ
170	Ⓐ Ⓑ Ⓒ Ⓓ

No.	ANSWER A B C D
171	Ⓐ Ⓑ Ⓒ Ⓓ
172	Ⓐ Ⓑ Ⓒ Ⓓ
173	Ⓐ Ⓑ Ⓒ Ⓓ
174	Ⓐ Ⓑ Ⓒ Ⓓ
175	Ⓐ Ⓑ Ⓒ Ⓓ
176	Ⓐ Ⓑ Ⓒ Ⓓ
177	Ⓐ Ⓑ Ⓒ Ⓓ
178	Ⓐ Ⓑ Ⓒ Ⓓ
179	Ⓐ Ⓑ Ⓒ Ⓓ
180	Ⓐ Ⓑ Ⓒ Ⓓ

No.	ANSWER A B C D
181	Ⓐ Ⓑ Ⓒ Ⓓ
182	Ⓐ Ⓑ Ⓒ Ⓓ
183	Ⓐ Ⓑ Ⓒ Ⓓ
184	Ⓐ Ⓑ Ⓒ Ⓓ
185	Ⓐ Ⓑ Ⓒ Ⓓ
186	Ⓐ Ⓑ Ⓒ Ⓓ
187	Ⓐ Ⓑ Ⓒ Ⓓ
188	Ⓐ Ⓑ Ⓒ Ⓓ
189	Ⓐ Ⓑ Ⓒ Ⓓ
190	Ⓐ Ⓑ Ⓒ Ⓓ

No.	ANSWER A B C D
191	Ⓐ Ⓑ Ⓒ Ⓓ
192	Ⓐ Ⓑ Ⓒ Ⓓ
193	Ⓐ Ⓑ Ⓒ Ⓓ
194	Ⓐ Ⓑ Ⓒ Ⓓ
195	Ⓐ Ⓑ Ⓒ Ⓓ
196	Ⓐ Ⓑ Ⓒ Ⓓ
197	Ⓐ Ⓑ Ⓒ Ⓓ
198	Ⓐ Ⓑ Ⓒ Ⓓ
199	Ⓐ Ⓑ Ⓒ Ⓓ
200	Ⓐ Ⓑ Ⓒ Ⓓ

「多益獎學金」申請辦法：

★凡向學習出版公司團訂New TOEIC Model Test課堂教材的同學，參加TOEIC測驗，成績達下列標準，可申請以下獎學金。

分　數	獎　學　金
990分滿分	2萬元現金支票
950分以上	1萬元現金支票
900分以上	5,000元現金支票
800分以上	1,000元現金支票
700分以上	500元現金支票

1. 同一級分獎學金，不得重複申請；申請第二次獎學金時，則須先扣除已領取的部份，補足差額。
   例如：某生第一次參加多益測驗，得分825，可申請獎學金1,000元，之後第二次參加測驗，得分950，則某生可領取
   10,000元 – 1,000元 = 9,000元獎學金差額。

2. 若同學申請第一次獎學金後，考第二次成績比第一次差，雖仍達到申請獎學金標準，將不得再申請獎學金。

3. 申請同學須於上課期間，憑成績單申請，並有授課老師簽名。

【本活動於2021年12月31日截止】